TO LOVE ME IS TO LOVE THE SKIN I'M IN

Written by Stephanie Carter
Illustrated by Darya Obraztsova

Dedication

For my dad, Titus, who encouraged me to write

For my mom, Annita, and my sisters, Danielle
and Brittany, for always believing in me

To those who struggle with your image,
this book is for you. You are beautiful,
capable, loveable, and the world
needs the good you can do.

Deja turned this way, that way, and back again, inspecting herself in her full-length mirror. Today was her first day of fifth grade.

I hate this shirt! I look like a pumpkin! she thought. This was the fourth top she had tried on. Frustrated, she stomped to her bed and slumped across it.

"Aaargh!" Deja screamed into her pillow.

A knock on Deja's door startled her. The door creaked open.

In peeked Deja's older sister, Saraiya.

"Deja, are you all right? Mom asked me to come check on you—and I could hear you groaning from downstairs," she said. "It's almost time for school."

"Just leave without me," Deja replied. "I can't go outside like this."

"What do you mean, Deja?" Saraiya asked.

"Look at me—I'm ugly!" She pointed at her hair and shirt. "I'm too fat, my hair is nappy, and my skin is too dark to wear this orange shirt."

Deja pointed to her phone. On the screen was the article, "This Year's Most Beautiful Girls".

"I will never be as beautiful as these girls."

Saraiya glanced at the magazine cover. On it were three young girls. They were petite and of light complexion. Each had wavy or straight hair.

Tears welled in Deja's eyes.

    Saraiya's tears began to well up in response, but Deja didn't see.

    "I'll be right back," Saraiya said, and she stepped out of the room. After a few seconds, she returned with her cell phone. She sat beside Deja on the bed.

Saraiya gently placed her hand on Deja's back.
   "Sis," she said, "You are beautiful and intelligent just as you are."
   "But I know how you feel."
Deja wiped her tears. "You do?"
Saraiya's eyebrows lifted. "I was once in your shoes."
Saraiya met Deja's eyes.

"But you always seem so sure of yourself," said Deja, disbelieving.

Saraiya replied, "It took a lot of work for me to believe in myself."

She squeezed Deja's shoulder. "Sit up for a minute, I want to share a story with you about one day in school that was very hard for me."

"What happened?" asked Deja.

Saraiya took a deep breath.

"During recess," she began, "my class was assigned to play kickball. My teacher had told us the day before we'd be allowed to pick our own teammates." Saraiya wrung her hands in her lap.

She continued, "I was nervous about going to school. I was the nerdy kid—now I know that nerds are cool, but then I didn't have many friends. That morning I too cycled through many outfits for school. I hoped that maybe if I looked nice, the kids would pick me as their teammate.

"I found something wrong with every piece of clothing I tried." Saraiya looked Deja in the eyes.

"I understand now that it wasn't the clothing at all. It didn't make one bit of difference what clothes I was wearing. Because I felt ugly inside, nothing I wore on the outside looked pretty to me." Saraiya paused to take a breath, then continued.

"I wondered if my skin color was the problem, because I only saw dark-skinned women in reality TV shows or in music videos. Neither of those spotlighted the beauty and brainpower Black women have.

"Light-skinned people seemed to lead most politics, TV, and history."

Saraiya continued, "Aside from Mom, I didn't have anyone else to look up to who looked like me."

Saraiya reached for Deja's hand and continued. "Eventually, mom called and said it was time to go to school. I settled with a ponytail and the pink jacket I was wearing."

"At recess, my fears came true. No one picked me.

"As I stood there alone, the last student in need of a team, I kept a straight face, but inside I was fighting the urge to cry. I began asking God why he cursed me with wide hips, wild coarse hair, and dark skin. Certainly, these had to be the reasons I was not chosen."

"I felt simply hopeless."

A smile spread across Saraiya's face. "Then I felt a tap on my shoulder. I turned around and saw an older girl. I recognized her as my teacher's assistant, Angela. She said she had noticed my sadness and wanted to see if there was anything she could do to help."

"What did you say?" asked Deja.

Saraiya replied, "I explained to her what happened. Angela listened and then took out her cell phone. I watched as she started tapping buttons. She turned her phone to me and showed me a website that changed my life."

At this, Saraiya took out her own cell phone, typed in a website, and texted it to Deja.

It was the website for *EBONY*, a magazine written to highlight the successes and disparities amongst the Black community. The home page featured a story titled, "Modern African American Female Role Models."

"Now we have to get to school, but let's continue our conversation this afternoon," said Saraiya.

"Girls, we have to leave or else you will be late for school." Their mother now stood at the door.

"Right on time!" Deja said, winking at her big sister.

All that school day, Deja had to use great self-control
to not look at the website!

When they arrived home, Deja asked Saraiya, "I
have never seen this magazine before. Who are these women?"

"Sis, these are women who look like us and we can aspire
to be like," Saraiya replied.

"We need to be our own true selves, but when I learned about these women, I realized that I can be my best me, the Saraiya I'm designed to be.

"Too many of the stories the world has painted about dark-skinned women are not true. All women have brains and beauty," said Saraiya.

"I recognize some of these women," Deja said. "Can you tell me about them?"

"Of course!" replied Saraiya.

Just as Saraiya began to tell Deja about the women in the magazine, they heard a deep voice say, "Excuse me, ladies."

Deja and Saraiya turned to look at each other, bewildered. Who could be talking?

"Psst, over here. The mirror."

Saraiya and Deja walked suspiciously over to the mirror. Deja tapped the glass to see if the mirror would speak again.

"Ouch! That hurts," the mirror blurted.

The girls jumped back in shock.

"Deja, did you know your mirror can talk?" asked Saraiya.

Wide-eyed, Deja replied, "I had no idea."

"I overheard your conversation and I think I can help," said Mirror.

"Oh, really. How so?" asked Saraiya.

Mirror replied, "They do not call me the Magic Mirror of Mystique and Knowledge for nothing! Not only can I take you to see each of these women of color in person, I will also share with you their stories if you'd like me to. All you have to do is think of where you want to go, snap your fingers, and off we roll!"

Both Saraiya and Deja looked skeptical.

   The sisters looked at each other for confirmation and confidence. Saraiya said, "Don't worry Sis, we'll be together. This will be fun!"

   She grabbed Deja's hand before she lost her nerve and thought of where she wanted them to go. As soon as she snapped her fingers, the mirror's silvery pink surface oozed out, took them by the hands, and began whirling them to their destination.

When they landed, Mirror, Saraiya, and Deja were inside a large house bustling with people running here and there. Everyone looked as though they were heading to meetings or had just ended one. Saraiya noticed a sign on the door in front of them. It read MICHELLE OBAMA. Saraiya jumped up and down.

"Deja, we are in the White House! The President and the First Lady must be here! We've traveled back to somewhere between 2009 to 2017!" Saraiya moved toward the door.

"Wait until you see what's inside. Let's go! Follow me," said Mirror.

Holding hands, Deja and Saraiya passed through the office door behind Mirror. Saraiya couldn't believe her eyes. Before them at her desk sat Michelle Obama.

"Deja, this is Michelle Obama," the mirror began. "She is an attorney who graduated from Harvard Law School. As our country's first African American First Lady, she is in a position of power and her voice is heard. Her radiant smile and overflowing confidence are heightened by the color of her skin. Doesn't she look fabulous in that yellow dress?"

Saraiya squeezed her sister's hand as she anxiously waited for the mirror to continue.

"Michelle was recognized among the World's twenty-five most inspiring women.

"Not only that but Vanity Fair acknowledged her fashion sense. She made best-dressed list two years in a row," explained the mirror.

Deja stood in awe. A political leader and a role model rolled into one.

Saraiya snapped her fingers and they were off to another location.

Saraiya and Deja then traveled with the mirror to a film production studio.

Deja asked excitedly, "Who are we here to see?"

Saraiya pointed to a woman across the room. The mirror began, "This is Issa Rae. She is an actress, writer, and producer of the HBO series Insecure. She graduated from Stanford University."

Saraiya remarked, "I love the way she styles her hair naturally."

"Because of her African features, Issa Rae's hair texture allows her to style her hair in various ways," replied the mirror.

Deja exclaimed, "Just like her talents, her hair is versatile."

Saraiya snapped her fingers again.

Deja had always loved gymnastics. She could hardly imagine the fact that she and Saraiya next landed in the middle of an Olympics training gym.

Saraiya turned to her left and pointed. "Look, it's gymnast Simone Biles! She earned the title, *Team USA Female Olympic Athlete of Year in December 2015.* She holds the record for most World metals, and she's only 24 years old!"

Deja said, "I have always wanted to keep with gymnastics. I feel like I can now."

"She too has noticeable hips, like you Deja. It only adds to her beauty but is minimized by her faultless routine execution. Simone is an inspiring sports icon!" exclaimed Saraiya.

Mirror asked, "Did you know that Simone has been criticized several times because of her hair?"

"She is gorgeous and extremely talented. What could people possibly say bad about her?" asked Saraiya.

The mirror replied, "Many spoke badly about Simone for coming to events with messy hair or not having her edges laid down. She stood up for herself."

Mirror continued, "At 22 years of age, Simone partnered with Japanese beauty brand SK-II for the No Competition Campaign. Her intention is to inspire women to define what beauty means to them and not take part in toxic conversation with others who try to dictate what beauty is supposed to look like."

"Young, Black, strong, and gifted. What more can you ask?" exclaimed Deja.

Saraiya snapped her fingers again.

We mustn't forget those
who helped paved the way.

The Magic Mirror of Mystique and Knowledge next deposited the sisters at the National Museum of African American History and Culture; a Smithsonian Institution museum located on the National Mall in Washington DC.

Saraiya read from the wall, "We mustn't forget those who helped paved the way."

The mirror began, "Barbara Jordan was a lawyer and the first Southern African American woman elected to the United States House of Representatives. During her time as congresswoman, her strong speaking skills opened many doors."

Barbara C. Jordan

"Barbara was an advocate for civil rights and the first woman keynote speaker for Democratic National Convention." explained Mirror.

Deja responded, "I admire her bravery to stand up for what she believed in."

Saraiya chimed in, "Especially during a time when there were so few woman in this field, even fewer with dark skin."

Valerie Thomas

The mirror continued, "Equally amazing is Valerie Thomas, a NASA data analyst and physicist who invented the technology used to produce 3D movies."

"You mean the really stylish glasses I get to wear when I go to the movies that make it look like the characters are coming out of the TV screen?" asked Saraiya.

Mirror replied, "Yes, Valerie Thomas is responsible for being able to experience movies like that."

"That is so cool!" exclaimed Deja. "Science is one of my favorite subjects. I will ask my teacher if we can learn more about this in class."

Dr. Alexa Canady

Saraiya's outstretched finger pointed to another display on the wall to the right.

"Ah, yes. Let us not forget Dr. Alexa Canady, the first African-American female neurosurgeon," said the mirror.

Deja replied, "I can only imagine the challenges she faced as a dark-skinned Black woman of that time practicing medicine. What an accomplishment! I want to leave a legacy like that one day too."

"I never knew about these women. I am so amazed," said Deja.

Saraiya snapped her fingers once more. This time, the girls found themselves back in Deja's room.

"Wow, that was so incredible! Thank you Mirror for taking my sister and me on that journey! There are so many beautiful and talented dark-skinned women. I want to be great like them," said Deja.

"Sis, you are already great," said Saraiya. "And rather than be just like them, you need to be the best you that you can be. You were born for greatness Deja!"

"But how do I get there?" asked Deja.

"It starts by loving who you are. By recognizing your strength even in what you may see as flaws," offered Saraiya.

"When you wake up each morning, look in the mirror and tell yourself you are beautiful and smart. Then find the school subjects you enjoy and pour yourself into them. Who knows what you might invent, or discover, or cure, or change, or grow!" urged Saraiya.

Saraiya smiled and then pulled back. "Wait, I didn't finish my story from earlier."

Deja looked at her sister. "Go on," she said eagerly.

"After Angela showed me the website for *EBONY* magazine," Saraiya continued, "she invited me to go with her to Girl Empowerment, an afterschool program. Angela is a volunteer there.

"I joined the program and it helped me learn to love myself and discover the good I can do. Because of her and the other women in the program, I grew a confidence I never knew was possible. Now that I am older, I volunteer at the program. Tomorrow, I want you to join me there after school," said Saraiya.

Deja smiled. "I would love to."

Deja quickly hugged Saraiya, then grabbed her backpack to get it ready for the next school day.

She took a final glance in the mirror, confident in her orange shirt and her afro. Grinning from ear to ear, she said, "I look flawless." Deja skipped down the stairs in excitement, optimistic for the future.

The End

Stephanie Carter is a children's book author with a background in Civil Engineering.
She resides in California's Inland Empire with her mother, two younger sisters and two nephews. Stephanie is a manager for one of the largest general contractors in construction. Within the company she works for, Stephanie serves as one of the founding members and lead recruiters of their internal Black Network organization.

Her role in recruiting involves training, outreach, professional interviewing, resume review, writing, and editing. Stephanie has been featured on two episodes of LPDcast, which is a Leadership & Professional Development podcast for First-Gen Students of Color. She wrote this book to help young kids appreciate their natural beauty and know their achievements are not limited by the way they look. Stephanie hopes this book will spark conversation about colorism and how to embrace who we are.

To Read More

Michelle Obama

Biography.com Editors. "Michelle Obama Biography."

https://www.biography.com/us-first-lady/michelle-obama

A&E Television Networks, 02 Apr. 2014. Edited 05 Nov. 2020. Whitehouse.gov. "Michelle Obama."

https://www.whitehouse.gov/about-the-white-house/first-ladies/michelle-obama/

Issa Rae

Imbd.com. "Issa Rae." https://www.imdb.com/name/nm4793987/bio?ref_=nm_ov_bio_sm

Simone Biles

Simonebiles.com. "Biography." https://www.simonebiles.com/bio

Team USA. "Simone Biles Artistic Gymnastics."

https://www.teamusa.org/usa-gymnastics/athletes/simone-biles

United States Olympic & Paralympic Committee, 2020.

Greaves, Kayla. "Simone Biles Will Never Change Her Hair for Anybody — Especially the Trolls."

https://www.instyle.com/beauty/simone-biles-hair. Updated 14 Feb. 2020.

Barbara Jordan

History.com Editors. "Barbara C. Jordan." History,

https://www.history.com/topics/black-history/barbara-c-jordan

A&E Television Networks, 09 Nov. 2009. Updated 12 May 2020.

Chicago - Alexander, Kerri Lee. "Barbara Jordan." National Women's History Museum. 2019.

www.womenshistory.org/education-resources/biographies/barbara-jordan

Valerie Thomas

Biography.com Editors. "Valerie Thomas Biography."

The Biography.com Website, https://www.biography.com/scientist/valerie-thomas

A&E Television Networks, 02 Apr. 2014. Updated 06 Mar. 2020.

Dr. Alexa Canady

Biography.com Editors. "Alexa Canady Biography."

The Biography.com Website, https://www.biography.com/scientist/alexa-canady

A&E Television Networks, 02 Apr. 2014. Updated 03 Sep. 2020.

Made in the USA
Las Vegas, NV
05 August 2021

27590722R00026